Parker Rogers

The Flowering Soul

written by
BARBARA BJORGE

authorHOUSE®

AuthorHouse™
1663 Liberty Drive, Suite 200
Bloomington, IN 47403
www.authorhouse.com
Phone: 1-800-839-8640

First published by AuthorHouse   4/14/2008

ISBN: 978-1-4343-4765-7 (sc)

Printed in the United States of America
Bloomington, Indiana

This book is printed on acid-free paper.

As I read this book and look back over the years that it covered, it makes me wonder if other young women are also enduring such pain as I was. I want to say…"hang on" , "it will get better" …I promise!

God's timing is not our timing, but His promises always prove true!!

God Bless You!!!

Take a
            Rosebud
and cup it gently...
            hold it
                        tenderly
            tend it
                        softly.
It's fragile
            and delicate.
Breath in
            it's fragrance
            caress it's
                        aroma
            exult it's
                        uniqueness
            ...but...
Guard it diligently...
            one thoughtless
                        grasping hand
            can crush and destroy
                        it's beauty
            can stamp out
                        it's glory.
            ...so...
Take a
            rosebud
and cherish it
            lovingly
...then...
Take a
            human heart
and cup it gently...
...and remember
            the rosebud!

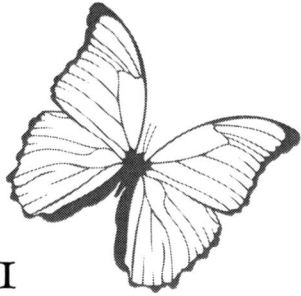

CHAPTER 1
THE BEGINNING
THE FIRST 15 YEARS

You make me so happy..
   your smile
      your touch
         your love.
You make my life
   worth the living
I love your voice,
   your hands,
      your eyes
   when they crinkle.
I love your spirit
   your freedom
      your caring ways
My prayer for you is
   that I can make you
      as happy
   as you always
      make me!

I give to you
    a heart of love;
  hold it gently.
I give to you
    my hopes and dreams
  treat them kindly.
All I have
    I entrust
      to your care.
Please, honor that.
I give to you
    the power
      to help me grow
  or
      to destroy my soul.
I give to you
    my trust
    and my faith.
It's yours to do with
    as you will.
Please be kind…
  Try not to hurt me
      because….
      …I really love you!

So many times
    I take you for granted;
  forgetting to treat you
      as the treasure
            you are.
I often forget
      to hug you
        and tell you…
  "I love you"
      "You're special"
        "I'm proud of you!"
Forgive me ,honey
      and remember always…
You are more precious
                    to me
      than life itself!

Why do my arms
   feel so empty
      and cold?...
Is it because there's no baby to hold?
And why do my eyes smart
   with tears
      yet unshed?...
Is it because of a dream that is dead?
And why does my heart
   feel so bruised
      and so battered?...
Is it because of loves hope that's been shattered?
When will it leave
   this great throbbing pain
And when will the sun
   start shining again?
Tell me, and give me some hope to go on,
Please tell me
   ....when is this emptiness gone?

"As soon as to me, you give all your strife
   and remember that "I" am the author of life.
Your dreams is not finished, it waits for you still
   follow Me, be patient, and trust in My will.
There's nothing that happens, that I don't control
   give me your heart, I'll again make it whole.
I'll give you my peace, I'll take all your sorrow
   You'll grow through this pain and you'll smile tomorrow.

I'm so afraid
    that someday
  you'll stop
    loving me,
and then
    the harder I try
  to hold you
    close to me…
  the father
  you seem
         away.
I want to
  let go,
but I'm so afraid…
    you'll ignore me,
        forget me,
           stop caring.
I'm sorry
  if I've clutched
    too tightly
    & hurt you;
I never meant to.
It's just that
    I'm so afraid
    of
      losing you….

Is it so hard
    to understand
            someone else's needs?
Or is it
    easier
    to
        ignore them?
Maybe they'll
            go away...
    Complain..
            ..call names;
        say
        "well
                are you still
                        miserable!"

"YES"
I hurt,
    I have needs too,..
                that aren't
                        being met.
I hurt!
    Can't you see?
                Don't you understand?
                        Don't you care?
It won't just
            go away.
I hurt!
    I need you!
Please listen!

Do you
    realize
    little one
what a blessing
    you
            are?
You
    make
        me
                feel
…needed
    …special
like you really
        need me
like you really
        love me.

Sometimes
    I resent
        giving up
            my youth
my fast
    slipping away
            time.
I'm sorry
    for that
    because you
        bless me.   (continue on next page)

To be
    needed
    ...special
        to
        someone...
what else
  is life
    about?
Will you too
  grow up
     and
        away
            from me
needing only
outward things
    and
not me?

I need you
    to
        need
      me
You make me
        special
           and
            important.

Kiss my brow, sing softly to me
of days gone past........
    before I was
of flowers & trees& brooks of satin
of lovers dreams...........
    and hopes to come.

Caress my cheek, sighing softly and gentle
& tell of life
    that I don't know
of fairies & elves and fantasies all
of stars that twinkle and lambs that low.

Tell me of dreams that really happen
    of wishes............
        that on stars come true

a rhyme, a poem, a cotton lullaby
a cloud to sleep on........
        snuggled by you.

Put your arms
        around me…
Tell me
        you love me…
not just with words
        but from
                your heart.
Hold me dear…
    let your soul
        speak to mine;
Words are nothing
    if they're not
        from within.
Touch me…
    love me…
Let me feel
        special and important
                to you.
Is that
        so very hard?
I guess
        it is…..

Silent longings
    deep needs
        tired of pleading
            &
            silently begging.
Take me away
    Be my
            Prince Charming
Let me be
            Cinderella
        for
            a night.
Take me away
    from the
            drudgery....
Give me
    ...romance
            excitement.
Let me feel
    ...special...
Take me away
    just one night
            once in awhile....
Take me away
    from it all
            & let me be
...a
    Princess....

Lord
    I'm really
        discouraged!!
Sometimes
    a messy house
        is
           a millstone
              of
                FRUSTRATION
I
    pick up
      …clean up
      ….tidy up
      turn around
           ---DISORDER---
Lord
    help me
    not be
        so overwhelmed
    by the
        mountains of
           mundaness.
Lord
    help me
        tackle things
    …positively
      …practically
        &
    help me
        become
Queen
    of
      this
        castle!

So much to see
    …to do
And we trudge through
    this short span

        …….unaware

    clothed in un consciousness

        dreary existence
    yet afraid

                to change…………

Maybe
    it's all we deserve
                after all.

You live
    in your world
  & I live
    in mine.
We try
    to unite them
            into one...
mine of dreams
    & fantasys
yours of logic
    & reason....
we bring them
            together.
Can our worlds
    be welded
            into one
    or
will they collide...
    destroying one of us
    or maybe both?...
Is it worth
    the risk...
    or is it
    already
    too late?

Being a housewife
　　is not easy!
　　It's a lot
　　　of work
　　&
　　It's emotionally
　　　　　harrowing…

You are
　　　stimulated…
　　you meet and talk
　　　to people
　　　all day;
You work
　　　and
　　come home
　　　　　to relax.

I meet needs
　　　　　all day
I do
　　boring things
　　day
　　　　after
　　　　　　day
　　　　　　　after
　　　　　　　　　day　(continue on next page)

repetitious things…
    over
      and
        over…
children crying
    ..fighting
dinner to make
house to clean
  dishes to wash
BORING!
   No Stimulation…
I work all day too…
But where
   do I go
  when I'm finished?
Where do I go
   to relax?

You
    ask

        me

            how

                I

                    feel?

Lonely,
    afraid,

        confused.,
wondering if
    I'll

        make

            it....
Hurt,
    wounded,

        & scared.
wanting to say...
    ...help me

        love me

            accept me

You
    ask

        me

            how

                I

                    feel?
I say
    "Fine thankyou,

        &

            you?"

A piece
    of
        my
            heart…
A slab
    of
        my
            soul…
a shoulder
    to
        cry on…
    a life
        to
            depend on.
Bit by bit
    piece by piece
  I give
    it away…
Will there be
  anything left
    for me?…
    or
        will I be
            all
                gone.
    bit by bit
        piece by piece
until
    nothings
            left?

Lord,
    I always seem to be messing up;
        saying the wrong things
            thinking wrong thoughts
                and having wrong
motives.
Lord,
    I really desired
        to be a spiritual GIANT
            a clean and holy vessel,
                pure of heart and
mind;
    someone you could be proud of!

Yet I seem to end up
    a grote§que
        dwarf...
unable to meet
           my own standards;
    feeling unfit and soiled.

And Lord
    though I know in my heart
    that I'm saved wholly by grace
        and my fare
           has been paid in full;
    I still feel inadequate and unworthy
        ...continuously letting you down,
and that somehow
        I've nailed you to that cross
           over and over again!

Lord
    I did it again
        thinking the worst
            instead
    of expecting
        the best.
I asked forgiveness, Lord
    but does that
        erase the pain
            of unbelief?

Help me Father
    to always expect
        the best
    and to see
        only the goodness
            in people.

Teach me Lord
    not to hurt others
        by my
            doubts and fears,
    even if it means
        the chance
        of being hurt
            myself.

Sometimes
    it's so
        confusing,
I feel like
    a lost ship
        in a RAGING storm
    with no home port
        in sight.
God,
    You are
        the author of life
            ....You know me
In your mercy
        and compassion
    help me to know
        and understand
            me too.
Bring me in
    to solid ground!

Caught
in the middle
..surrounded
..crowded
..misunderstood.
So much potential
…where to put it?
Not having
the freedom
of the oldest
nor
the indulgences
of the youngest.
Being
…just
there…
Lord,
Please help me
to remember
to show her
how unique
and special
she really is.
Help me
to remember
to take time
for just her.
Don't let me
forget her
special needs.

(continue on next page)

Please help me to
   to make sure
     she never feels like
just one of the
         crowd…
the one
   ..stuck in the
         middle…

I want to do
        great things, kind things,
                wonderful things
        then everyone will love me.
But
    I try too hard
    and things never go
                the way I want them to
    and I think
                nobody can love me.

Teach me Lord
        not to believe that
                I always have to earn love
        and that
                I never can quite make it.
Teach me that love is
        given freely
                for no apparent reason
….at least
        that's what I'm told Lord
                Is it true?

My Son...
    I have
       such dreams
    for you,
       such high hopes.
I want
    for you
all that's
    best!
My heart
    tears
when I see
    you do things
    I know
    will hurt you.
I want
    so badly
    to save you
from lifes pains.
Don't you know
    how much
    I love you?
Can't you stop...
    and listen...
and trust
    in my judgements
       sometimes?

I want
    you to grow,
to be
    independent,
    to be a man
       in your own right
       ...but ...
You're still
    my son
    and
I want
    to help.
Won't you
    please
       let me.

Little boxes
    closing me in,
jail cells clanging
    turmoil within.

Prison of words,
        and rules
        and hate
who's right...or wrong
Who chooses
                our fate?

Are choices ours...
    chances to
                decide?
or bred
    deep within us
...others rules to abide?
Little boxes
    holding me down
freedom a myth
    thorns for
        my crown....
Little boxes
    closing me in,
no escape
    just an echoing
        ...din....

Wisps of
    fantasy
invading the mind.
Vague imaginations
    soaring on
        wings of dreams.
Fairy tale panoramas
    invaded by
        stark realities;
But.....
   which is truth?...
    the dreamer
        sleeping
   or the
    awakened automat?
Banishment of fantasy
    or
    discardment of reason...
Is truth
    even
      truth?....
   or is it only
wisps of
    fantasy...
    after all.

Oh God.
    I want
      so
     <u>badley</u>
to be free....
I feel
    a wildness
      within me....
erratic gypsy blood.
I push it down
        d
          o
            w
              n
cover it...
    hide it...
pretend it doesn't
        exist..
but
  it bubbles on.
To be free,
  to run wild,
Just once to do
    just
     for me.
To not <u>have</u> <u>to</u>...
Oh God,
  What is wrong
    with me?
Other people
    adjust.

(continue on next page)

Other people
　　　aren't always
　　　　　seeking rainbows.
They find
　　contentment and peace.
You promised that
　　　　Lord,
　　and yet I can't
　　propagate it
　　　　　for me.
Help me, God
　　please
I'm tired......
Change my
　　heart,
　　　　Lord...
Make me content.
Stop this
　　wildness...
this gypsy blood.
　　from boiling.

Do you love me?

I'm here aren't I.

Do you need me?

Have I ever said I didn't.....

But I need to hear it.......

Then listen to yourself!

Hey!!!

Where are you going?

I've found a new love

But why?

He loves me and needs me

But so do I

OH.........

You never told me...........

CHAPTER 2
FALLING IN LOVE

I
  met
     a
  man
with coal-black hair
  and
    sea-blue eyes.
"Come"
    said he
" We'll sail
      the stars
    & swim
        the dipper,
catch
    moonbeams
    & slide
      the rainbow!"
I
  loved
    a
       man
  with raven hair
  and
  azure eyes;
who went to the land
  of dreams
      …where fairies dance
    and
       dragons sit,
[under mushroom caps,
    playing love songs]
    ….and I?....
I went home
  and
  washed the dishes
  and
  swept the floor.

I look at you
　and my heart beats
　　a little faster…

I like to be near you…
I don't understand
　　what's happening….
　　　Why do I feel this way?
I've never felt this way
　　　　before.

What do I want
…..a friend
　….a lover
　　what?
I'm drawn to you
　in a way I've never
　　experienced.
I don't know what's happening…..
　　or what to do
　　　　about it…
Why do you have
so much effect
　on me?
What is happening?!!

In a
    little world
  where no one lived
    but you and I
    we loved
We danced
    to such beautiful music
  the world
    couldn't have heard
        anyway.
In our
  little world
    …all alone…
  we sang with twilight
      &
    kissed the wind,
  we dreamt
    with the poets.
In a
  little world
  where no one lived
    but you & I
  we listened
    to our heartbeats
      &
        we loved!

I want to
    touch you
        be with you…
I can't promise
           you anything
    except
        faith
           &
           truth
    &
      love
          beyond words.
In my heart
    we are one.

I don't expect
    you to promise
        me anything
    except
      to love me
  & allow me
    to love you

    ….for as long
        as is…

You encompass
    my mind
        my heart
            my passions.

Your presence abides
    in my
            Soul….

My love for you
    is an ebb-tide
        of
    endless flowing.

You fill me with
    uncontainable joy!

You touch
    my innermost being……

I really love you!!

Friend
  ...lover
  ...father
  ...brother...
A love
  transcending
    reason.
Space and time
    dissolved
    ... ad infinitum...
Can such as this
    ... last?
Or as
  the falling star
  blazing
    so brilliantly
    ...it burns itself
              out.
Can human hands
  hold
    eternity?

Each second
   we're apart
     seems
       an eternity.

Each hour
   we're together
     seems
       a second.

Let's make
   each second
       we share
   count so much
    that it lasts....

      forever!

You kiss me
and it hurts
so sweetly.
We walk away
from each other,
so many times,
and it hurts
so bitterly.
We hold each other
and it hurts
so tenderly.
Oh God....
I love you
so much...
and it hurts
so painfully!
We try
so hard
to let go
of each other,
and it
hurts ....
so badly!
Is this
what love is? ...
to hurt
so sweetly
you can't
let go ....

You have
    loved me
  & made me
    strong.
You held me
   &
    I reached
        the stars.
You sought me
   &
    I came
   &
    became.
Don't desert me, love
You were there
   & my life
      became complete;
   and all because
You loved me.

We
      hold hands …
      and
            walk
      and
            talk.
Sometimes
      we kiss
      and
        hold
      each other.
We share …
      our hopes
      and dreams,
our joys
      and pain.
We share …
      something
      so special
            and
      so wonderful …
It's almost
      frightening.
We know
      we shouldn't
      be together
      shouldn't
      feel this way ..
            but

(continue on next page)

We can't
    seem to
      let go …
   no matter
   how hard
     we try.
So
   we hold hands
   and walk
    and talk
and try not to think

Just once
    "please, oh please Lord!"
Just once
    in this
         cold empty world
of shattered dreams....
Just once
    "please"
      let fairy tales
            come true....
      let the impossible
               be....
      let there be
         a miracle....
Just once
    Lord
    "please, oh please!"

I opened my door
        and there
                you were.
We promised each other
        not to be together
                anymore
but there you were.
You held me
        in your arms ...
        and I couldn't stop
        trembling.
I miss you
        so much!
You held me,
        and my darkness
        became light again.
How many times
        we have tried
                to let each other go!
How many times ...
        we can't!
How many times
        will I open
                my door
and find you there ....
        and be so grateful
        to be with you
                one more time?

Tenderly enfolded
    in arms
        of love,
I hear you whisper...
        adoringly,
    and caress me
        gently,
    full of love.
Saying sweet truths
    I love to hear,
        and suddenly
I become a princess!
        a queen!,
the most beautiful
    woman
        in the world!
Is it possible
    not to love in return
someone
    who can transform a life
with a caress,
    a word,
      and love?

Well....
     we did it
          beloved.
We held hands
     and set out
     to follow our hearts.
We'd fought
               so hard
          against it...
and the struggles
               proved useless.
     so
     we decided to grab
                    our dream.
We set out
     so bravely
          until....
               reality struck...
a solid door
               of reason;
          smacking our faces...
          and we knew...
          ...we couldn't!
          ...to hurt
               so many
          ...happiness
          bought with pain...
...not our style.
So
     we never
          made it.
But at least
     we tried....

Two souls touching
for a brief moment in time …………

Two spirits welded together
in space ………

Two hearts
joined forever
by unseen forces
………..put away
and treasured
secretly

Will this heart
ever be whole again
on its own?

Will the two souls
ever separate?

Can one
survive
….alone……?

In the beautiful garden
  stood majestic trees
  and babbling brooks…
serenity and beauty ruled.
"Of all in this garden
  shalt thou partake"
    said God
"save this one tree."

The beautiful garden
  dimmed in view
  The brook babbled…silently
  and the sun shone
              unnoticed…
  for all they saw
    was the forbidden tree;
All else was
        distorted
          ..unseen
            ..unheeded.

"My child"
  said God
"I have given you a garden;
    full of my gifts and treasures
        for your enjoyment…
    and of all this garden
        you may partake
    ….save for this
        one tree."

(continue on next page)

"Oh God"
pray I
"Don't let me look so hard at the
     one forbidden tree, that I forget about the garden.
Let me enjoy the fruits and treasures you've given me
to partake of. Don't let me lose the garden for the sake
of one forbidden tree. Help me to take joy, in that which
you have chosen for me. Let me trust in your knowledge and
righteousness!"

Why does something
        So beautiful
Have to hurt
    so bad?
Why can't everything
    always turn out
            right & wonderful?

Why does pain
        have to be
        a part of joy?
Isn't anything in this world
        just a little
                perfect?
Sometimes I wish
        I could
        just jump off!
But then maybe
.........just maybe..........
            the joy makes it all
                worthwhile!

The cocoon
          was safe
                    and warm
A prison
     ...maybe...
     but still
               a havan.
It began to
     open
     .....
          sunlight
          filtered through
          ****
The butterfly
     raises her face
               her heart
     fluttering
               wildly
She pushes
     and stretches
               ...reaching
                    ...exploring

And then...
     ....she's free!
Spreading wings
     of abandon
she soars
     and swoops
Joyously
     embracing
               the wind

(continue on next page)

Fluttering wings
   and bursting
       heartbeats
she reaches toward
      the warmth
  ....the sun....
ascending higher
  and higher
   ....ecstacy!
Her dream
    within
      her grasp!
Then...
  as it
    barely begins.
  it
    ends
and
  ....she
  dies.

CHAPTER 3
GOING FORWARD

Afraid
    to live.
Afraid
    to die.
Lost in a world
    of pain
        & confusion.
Wondering why the mind
    won't just slip
        into neutral
    &
        let me be!
   …Peace
      at
         least…
OH GOD
I cry
    in desperation!
I'm lost
    ….alone
      ….searching.
Help me Lord
    not to be afraid
    --- to live
        or
        to die.
PLEASE GOD
   …give me
      peace…

I
  had
        a
     love
who
       went away.
I
  held
          a
     dream
  that died.
The star
      burnt out
   in the palm
             of
                 my hand.
Oh God
    give me
        your grace
    to pull myself
                up again…
      to stand
                straight
                      &
                         tall
      on my feet
                again,
      and
          give me
             the courage
      to
        reach out
               &
      try
         and
            grab
               that star again!

60

Chaotic
   confusion
  mind-boggled
   mass of
        mystery…
Who knows
   the heart
    but you, God
  you
   who seems
       so far away ---
I'm a tangled twist
      of
       misconceptions!
Show me
   the way!
Show me
   God…
  for you,
   only you,
    know my
      heart!

Today was
     so
        hard!
My insides
     were
splitting apart;
I missed you
          so much…
   I ached all over!
I don't know whether
          I'll survive
             or
           lose my mind.
I'm so tired
     of fighting ---
   I'm just so tired----
I hope it's
     worth it.

Satiny velvet
    world of dreams…
Silky soft
    feather clouds
        of fantasy…
Warmth
    and
      peace…..
---§HATTERED---
By §pears
    of
      morning light.
PIERCING
      SCHREECHING
          GLARE!

Oh please, don't go away
   caressing shangrelah
      of dreams..
   wait for me….
      I'll be back.

I try so hard
    to have no hope…
I crush my dreams
        with unrelenting fists.
I'm afraid to allow
      optimistic
          rays of imagination
      into my mind.
I care too much
   My wound is to tender.
If I hope
   If I dream
and I lose again
I might not
     survive.
The pain has been
       too much
         too destructive
          too soul-searching
And yet…
It's always there.
It's tentacles creeping,
        seeping
          in.
A flash of
   ….maybe
    ….what if?....
Then
   I crush it!
    I stamp on it!
I want no hope,
   I need no dreams
    --do I?--

Where are you, my darling?
  I feel the gentle touch
    of your thoughts;
  they caress my mind
  ....but leave........
    aching emptiness.

I miss you
    so much.
I am away from you
  but you are always
          with me.
My love for you
    an eternal circle.
Wherever you are,
          my Darling,
    my heart
          is with you!

In the stillness of the night
    when strivings cease
        and dreams soar
      on winged abandon…….
I feel your hand caress my cheek
    ……..your lips
        brush my brow
My soul
    reaches for you………..

"NO"

In daylight glare
      reality reigning……………

This cannot be!
  This should not be!
  This will not be!

I KNOW! I KNOW!

…… BUT……

In the stillness of the night……………

66

Lord,
  I really thought
    that time was supposed to be
      a great healer;
  that the pain
     would lessen
   somehow become
     less real…
  but it doesn't….
It stabs my insides
     …unending
     …aching
       …throbbing.
Oh Lord
  I've tried…
  you know I have…
  but I can't
     do it,
  I can't
     handle it,
Please
  do it for me!
Take away
  this ever-abiding
  agony of heart.
If time heals
  speed it up..
 and if it doesn't
then…
  stop my heart.

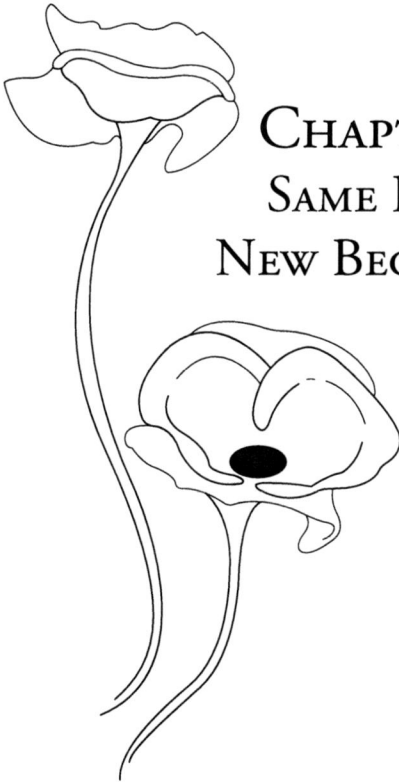

CHAPTER 4
SAME PLACE
NEW BEGINNING

The princess
   never
      smiled
because
   she
      knew
if she
   smiled
the kingdom
 "which
    she
       loved"
would
   f
     a
       l
       l
  a a t!
   p r
But
  one day
  a handsome
         prince
           came;
and she
  couldn't
      help it
She
  ….smiled….
  and
   the kingdom
        still
         stood,

(continue on next page)

it just
  shook
        a
          lot!
so
  the princess
    continued
            to smile.
But
  she was careful
    that she never
            laughed
because
    she
        knew
if she
      laughed
the
    kingdom would
          f
            a
              l
                l
a a t
  p r
  ....surely....

A new life
     starting over
…renewed commitment
     …brand new avenues.
Putting all
     to the alter
Trusting God
     and "His" ways.
Holding nothing back
     for security.
So hopeful…
     …yet full
               of fears.
Oh God,
  let it be good
     and right
  and make it
          work
     this time…..

Where
    did
        it
            go?
...the beating heart
    ...the racing pulse
        ...the kiss
                that seared the soul.
When did we
    let it loose?
Where is it hidden
                within us?
Come my love
    let's search
                our depths
    and find it
                again....
And when we do
    we'll never,
                ever
    let it slip away
                again!

My love
    is deepening
    ….I think….
It's confusing….

I've been with you
            so long
    I'm not sure…
        where commitment ends
        & love
                begins.
I pray
    and ask God
    to let my love grow
        and become
                    real to me
        like it used to be.
I think it is….
I'm not sure
    I'm really confused,
But I do think
            it's coming…

So confused
    so scared
Caught in a labyrinth
                of fears.
Wanting change
    but clinging
                to security.
Wanting to make choices
    but unsure of
        how....
            or even what.
Not sure of
    my own heart
                or mind.
Wondering if
    everyone else
    ever feels like this
    or is it
        just me?
The mind
    in circles
    so confusing...

I wish I could
    just
        shut myself off!

I love him…
You know
I do…
but over the years
it's been
so strangled
and it's not
the same.
I know
it can grow again
if it's
given a chance
but it's like
starting from scratch
and it's hard…..
Please God
let me love him again
the way
I used to
the way
I should…..

Please!

Inner turmoil
  swirling dust storm
      fogged emotions.
Digging deep
  hoping to discover
  the root-bound
          depths
      of
          discontentment.
War-torn psyche
  scarred over
      sub-conscience
Knowing somehow
  the answer waits
      ...somewhere
              within....

Oh Lord
 it
 really
   hurts!
I feel like
 …an alien
  …an outcast
 …alone…
I've failed Lord
 made mistakes
  and
 I'm sorry!
Is there no compassion?
   no understanding?
  just
   COLD, JUDGING
     hearts?
Is there no forgiveness;
 Is everyone else
    so perfect
 they've never
    fallen?
Oh Lord…
 Let your forgiveness flow.
From me
 to them
 from them to
   me
 from you
   to all.
Give me your
  healing balm, Lord;
 so it
  doesn't hurt
    anymore!

So sheltered,
    and so protected;
You've never had to face
    the real world.
You've never been surrounded
        by fiery
                arrows of doubt.
How can you
            comprehend me
                ...you're world's away.
We have
    no common ground
                to meet on.
I really hope
    you never have to leave
            your rose-colored world...
    I hope reality
            never confronts you.
My world would be too hard
    for you
        to survive in.

Oh God of love
   --are you?—
Are your hands
        spread out
            in forgiveness.
    or is vengeance
     your forte?
Is the wisdom I have
        [though tiny]
  from your spirit
   or
    my humanity…
    & if so…
Do you
   understand
       with compassion ---
   or chastise
     with a fury?
Have I a mind
   to learn
  or do I follow blindly
   the way of men
    who claim knowledge
        from you?
Give me truth
  oh God of love
    ---or
   are you?---

Little
    pat
    answers…
so easy
    to give,
nice little truisms
  on how
I should live.
A pat
  on the head
  a surfacy smile…
then step out
    of my world,
  forget
    for awhile.
But I can't leave
  I've nowhere
    to go;
If there really are
    answers…
I'd SURE LIKE
    to know.
Your little retorts
  don't help me
    at all
you say "be strong!"
  I'm starting
    to fall.
So if you care…
  in any
    small way…
It's what you do

(continue on next page)

that matters…
not words
that you say.
Your little
pat
answers
are easy to share
But to be part of my
WORLD,
You really should
…. care…

World of emotion…
    and
    earth of reason
You rage against
           each other…
Battling
    bitterly…
You gnaw
     at my insides.
Ferousiously
     you attack!
Trying to destroy
    each other.
Will it
    never
        end?…
    this war of destruction
    this Armeggeden battlefield.
Oh…peace and tranquility…
    how I desire you!
But…
    I don't know how
       to claim you…
    to possess   you…
    without destroying a part
        of myself.
Emotion and reason
    fighting each other
not able to exist
    without the other
or with the other.
Oh how confused I am!

I am alone
   no one speaks to me
      I hear nothing.........

I wait
   In
     vast, empty
       spaces

         and weep............

My voice
  echoes
 in hollow wastelands

   desolation
     is my
       home.

There is nothing......

There is no-one......

   and

   I weep.

Why
       are
       you crying?
You have
          the world
by the tail
Hey----
    your husband
      doesn't cheat…
    your kids
      are healthy…
    your house is big
        &
    your car
        runs
What more
         could you
                    want?
Hey----
    I'll
      buy you
            another beer
      &
you can
    tell me
…why
    are
         you crying?
         ****

(continue on next page)

86

I'M crying
        for a
    wish
    on
            a
                star
    …that
        never came
    &
    a dream
        that
                died……..

SURROUNDED
           by people
        …all alone…
wanting a friend—
--someone to touch—
             to sooth
                    my soul.
…yet I'm
     all alone…
Ultimatly
     it doesn't matter
          who's around…
I'm surrounded
              by people
      yet
…all alone…

It's an
     empty
     world
filled with
          confusion.
Cold
     &
     Dark.
The mind
     a maze
          of
          dead-end
               streets.
Wide open
     roads
     ending in
     cul-du-sacs.
Trapped
     in cages
with
          no
          doors.
It's an
     empty
     world
with no way
               out
     but
     dreams that
     fade....
          leaving voids
     of

(continue on next page)

lonliness.
It's an
empty
World with no
escape
but dreams
that
desolve.

Into the night
    I fly.
A soul set free.
   Soaring on wings
        of freedom
     unfettered, unabandoned
     I fly!
The wind caresses my face.
   The sweet fresh smell
        of new mown hay
          in my nostrils
    I fly.
   Through clouds
    of glossimer cotton
    Swooping over mountains
        far below....
    I fly..
Oh... How wonderful
   How free
   How exhilarating
   I fly!!

I give it
    to you Lord
…my hurts
  …my fears
all the things I
    try to cling to
    & know I shouldn't.
I'll probably try
  to grab it
        all back…
…please don't let me.
Please, Lord
  hold me
      and care for me.
I'm weak
      & wounded,
  …give me strength
    and support me;
hold me
    by your hand
until I can
    stand again
    …not alone….
but in
      your strength.
Right now
  I'm too tired
    and beaten
    to do anything…
    but
    …give it all
          to you.

Restoration hast thou promised me
that I'll be built, oh God, by thee.
Not by the flesh, shall this temple be;
but by thy Spirit, constructed of thee.

As the temple of Soloman, I did fall
torn asunder, left standing..not one wall.
but my soul, oh God, hast heard thy call
and new restoration, my cover, my shawl.

Here I am Lord
...scared
    and unsure...
but I know
    you are still
        in control.
I've been hurt
    a lot, Lord
and I've hurt
    others too
but you've shown me
    that
        you can heal...
Please do it Lord
    --quickly—
I've tried
    others things Lord
but without you
    ...it's hopeless.
Only your ways
    are peace.
I'll try hard Lord
    but I'm
        weak...
I need your strength
    to make it!
So please
    help me.
Please Lord...

I've got to do
    something....
Something
        positive
            &
                forward.
The world
    is closing in
        on me...
trapping me in
    a little box.
I have to escape
    before I
        suffocate.
I have to
    set a goal,
        step out,
            move ahead.
If I don't
    do something...
    I'm finished!
Lord
    Help me to get going
    Get me out of this
            apathy
I feel like I'm
        dying inside.
I've got to do something....

If I could have
    anything I wanted,
        in the whole world....
If I could
    make a wish,
        that would come true...
If just once...
    just once....
        ***
I'd see you
    walking down the street...
        towards me.
I'd look into
    your beautiful
        sky blue eyes.
I'd feel my heart warm
    at your special smile...
    you saved just for me.
I'd feel your arms
    around me...
    and try to keep my heart
    from bursting
        right through my chest
My whole world
    would be right
        again....
If only...
    just once,
        just once....
If I could have
    anything I wanted
        in the whole world.....

I think that if
    I wait long enough,
            hope hard enough,
                    believe strong enough.
I'll open my door
    or
    answer my phone
        or
    look out my window…
and you'll
    be there.
Somehow,
    someway,
You'll just
    be there…
If only
    I believe hard enough
            and
            wait long enough
and hope
    and believe
        and wait.....

"Things will change,"
　　　　you say
　"Give me another chance,
"I'll meet your needs."

Words
　　words
　　　　words
But things
　　haven't changed…
You haven't even tried
　　　to meet my needs.
All you can see
　　　　is yourself.
I feel cheated
　　lied to
　　　used.

　　WHAT
　is the use
　　　of even trying?..

I made
  a mistake.
I let my heart
  be touched
    by someone else …
  other than you.
And
  you have
    punished me,
  and
    punished me
      and
        punished me!
Every day
  I pay the price …
again and again …
  over and over…
will it
  ever end?
Will you ever feel
  that enough justice
    has been meted out
to satisfy you?
How long …
  How long
    will you exact payment
      from me?
I'm sorry.
I can't go back
  and change things,
How long
  before you're satisfied
    that I've paid enough?

  Ever?

Surface relationships
    hollow laughter
        searching for
        ....what!
Have
    a drink
        &
tell
    a joke
It doesn't matter
        if
        your brothers
            dying.
Nobody cares
        if
        the beaten child
            cries.
Have another drink
        and
        we'll all
            be friends.
Don't ask
        for truths
        &
don't remember me
        tomorrow----
Surface living
        requires little
            and
        hardly hurts
            at all!

What is truth
   and
   what is happiness?
Lord,
   I don't even know
      anymore
…if I ever
    even did.
My logic
   and
   my emotions
are eons apart.
I'm so tired of
   these head trips!
Only you, God
   really know
what truth
   and happiness
        are.
Please…
   for my
   peace of mind…
Let me know
    too.

Knowing I am
   a self-filled
        person;
   ruled by emotions
   unable to cope
   filled with depression…
   I can't overcome.
Dying inside
   …a slow death
  feeling like life
   is passing me by….
      …nothing done
      …nothing accomplished
  who really cares anyway?
Guilt piled
  on emotional strain.
God, oh God,
   where are you?
Iron gates are closing
     around me.
God,
   forgive me…
   I'm so self-centered,
   My will is not
     sufficient.
Help me
  grab your strength!
Let Jesus overcome me
  and
    shine through!

You look me
        in the eyes …
and lie to me.
You leave
        my bed
        and go to anothers
then convince me
        it's all
                my fault.
You turn me around
        so I don't know
                truth anymore.
I think
        I'm going
                crazy!
You are so nice …
        I feel so guilty.
Everything
        is my fault;
It can't be yours …
        you're too perfect,
                I'm too rotten.
You tell me
        it's my problem ,..
If only I would
        If only I could
                If only I were …
STOP THIS!
I can't
        stand it anymore!
Let me off this
        mind-destroying
                voyage
                        of destruction!
Please …
        Please …
Don't do this to me
        anymore!

We have a bond
        between us…
    that stretches
        space and time.
I really do
        love you;
    but I will not
        allow myself
    to let it be.
I cannot sit back
        and watch you
            destroy yourself.
I will not
        plant seeds
    that you will
        stamp out.
If you hurt
        yourself
    you hurt me..
and I'm not strong enough
        to handle that
    …and you are
        slaying yourself slowly.
If the bond
        we have
    means anything to you;
    and if you love me..
        STOP
… stop it now…
Please don't destroy
        yourself
    and everyone else
        who loves you.

Pretty little
    dresden doll
… so pretty…
You look
    so strong.
All painted up
    a smile
    on your face…
Nobody knows
    the tears
    inside.
Don't let them
    touch
    you…
  little dresden doll
    they might
    hold you
        too tight…
…they might
    hurt you
    and
    break you.
Be careful….
  pretty little
    dresden doll.

Topsy-turvy
　upside
　　down,
inside
　outside,
round and round.
The mind
　a chasm
　painful depths,
uncovered
　　dreams..
　awaiting yet.
seeking here
　searching there
wanting answers
　… somehow
　… somewhere.
Pin-dart
　　stabbings
　frantic
　　brain
… which way…
　…what time?....
destructive game.
Whirling
　　brain swirls
　mind
　　a din,
topsy-turvy
　world within.
Never quitting
　unending
　pain
　reach the surface
to sink
　again.

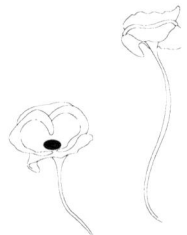

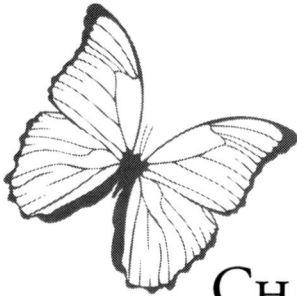

CHAPTER 5
THE DIVORCE

It
  doesn't
    matter
It's
    not
    true…
Tomorrow
    doesn't
       matter
I won't
    be there
       anyway
I won't
    let it
      come!
The heart
    is
    dead
      &
  the mind
      a
        chasm…
It
    doesn't matter
It's
    not
    real….

God,
    where are you?
Why are you
    so hard to find?
I'm confused and mixed up
    I know you're there somewhere...
They say you never move
    ---we do---
    but how do I get back
    to where you are again?
I have doubts Lord
    then feel guilty
    because I'm told
      you're not supposed to have doubts.
Everyone tells me
    this and that
    and I really think
      I try Lord
but I always seem to fail.
My faith is evaporating!
If you're there Lord
    please grab me
    and hang on
      TIGHT!
Don't let me go
    Please!
Oh God
    where are you?

Physically,
  spiritually,
    &
        emotionally
            BANKRUPT!
Trying so hard
    to grab
    Gods hand....
    to pull it
    all together.
Searching for
    firm ground
  to put my
    feet
        on.
Seeking for peace
    &
    the tranquility
    of soul.
....a new
        start...
....a new
        bankroll...
    to
    start over
    with.
Searching
    &
    hurting
    &
    searching....

Oh pain…
    release your
    iron grip…
my insides
            ache.
There's a big, empty
    cavity
    full of aching
                need.
It hurts
    so bad!
Release…
    where are you?
Peace
    comfort..
    will you forever
        elude my grasp?
Oh pain…
    release me
    soon…

Was it
     … all for naught
               Father?
Were
     all those years
               a waste?
I ran
     the race
…and lost,
     at the finish line.
Was I
     … a failure
     … too selfish
Did I not
     perservere
               or
     trust you
               enough?
Forgive me
     Father
     for where
          I lacked.
Let me have
     at least
          learnt
     and grown
through it all;
Please
     don't let it all
     have been
     for nothing
… a waste.

What
   happened
      Lord?
What
   happened?
Did I fail?
Did I
   do my best?
I
   really tried
                 Lord,
      at least....
         I think
            I did....
I read
      all the books,
      I tried
      all the tricks,
      but still....
         it
         never
                 worked....
What
   happened
   Lord?

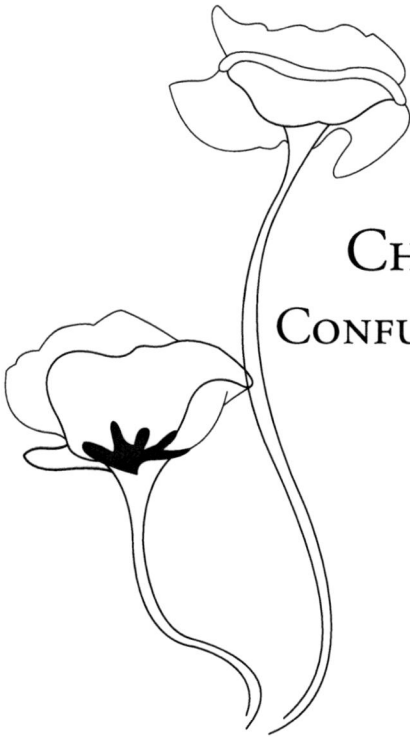

CHAPTER 6
CONFUSED CIRCLES

She died
    a long time
            ago.
…not
    physically…
    just
in every way
    that counts,
her dreams
    her hopes
        her lofty
        aspirations.
Now she walks,
    an empty shell
.. doing what
        must be done…
        ..caring for
        the ones
        who need caring for,
    ..passing through
    aimlessly,
When her body
    catches up,
and follows her spirit
        into death…
it will
        only be
    .. a formality ..
a uniting
    of her being;
because
She died
    a long time
    ago.

I know I shouldn't
    be doing this…
jumping into another
    marriage
    so soon.…
But I'm so afraid…
    the kids need a father.
    I don't know how
            to cope alone.
You're offering me
    a security
    I won't have
    by myself.…
and I'm scared to be
    …alone…
I really probably
    shouldn't do it
    but I'm so frightened
    and lonely…
    … I probably
            will.…

Hey little surprise…..
    I'm glad you're here!
I never expected
    such a precious gift.
You are
    a
        joy!
I must admit…
    you were quite
    an adjustment
    …but…
God knew…
    you were
            exactly what
    I needed most!
Hey little surprise….
    you
        sure
            were!
But you know what?
You're the very best
    and
    the very nicest
                surprise
I've
    ever
        had!

I think of
   presents
     and Santa
               and turkey.
I love
   buying gifts
and watching
   the snow fall,
seeing the kids
   excited faces
.... wondering what's in
     their
          brightly wrapped gifts.
I'm sorry Lord...
   I
     sometimes forget
     the real meaning
               of it all.
You gave us
     the greatest gift
               of all...
     the greatest gift
               there ever was....
and I think
     of
          trimmings.....

White stuff lying
    all over the ground
ice-nipping wind
    swirling around
bright baubly balls
    hang from the tree
lots of big presents
    waiting for me!

Pretty things glitter..
    they tempt me so much
I reach out to grab them
    but Mom says "don't touch!"

Silvery strands
    hand down from the tree
colored lights twinkle
    and winkle at me
A stocking is hanging
    Is that my name on,
I'm really not sure
    of what's going on.

Christmas is wonderful
    it's really such fun
for a sweet little guy
    who's just turning one.

It's all so exciting
    and tempting to me
I know I'll have great fun
    ...if mom doesn't see....

What's happened?
  Why have you changed
          so much?
Is it me?
  Do I bring out
    the worst
      in people?
Are the responsibilities
    too much?
  Is that what's happened?
I don't know
    what to do...
    what to say...
How do I
    help you?
I'm so confused...
Please tell me...
  what's happened?

Hang on…
   be patient…
     trust God…
   be firm…
be strong…
    stick it out…
     perservere…
hold it
   all together…
don't give up…
    be gentler…
     be selfless…
    submit….
be responsible…
   be
   TOUGH…
don't whine…
   don't cry….

Oh God…
   I am
  so°°°°
    tired
  so°°°°
     weary….
I can't
   hang on
   any
     longer.
Forgive me….
   I don't know
   what
     happened….

123

You just walk in one day
        and say
" I can't afford
        to support you
                anymore."....
    and walk out;
forgetting promises,
        commitments,
...copping out...
Then you say
        "please understand'.
                But
        ...I can't
        ...I don't.
I still have
        my commitments,
            my responsibilities;
and I don't walk out
                on them....
I couldn't...
        I wouldn't...
I'm sorry
        but
I really don't
        understand.

Hollow emptiness
in the pit
of my stomach,
Frozen panic
in my brain…
a familiar feeling..
Caught in
paralyzing fear
digging deep
for inner strength…
I know it's there
somewhere.
Hang on…
Have faith
… wait it out
pretend it's not there
and maybe
… it'll
disappear…
If only
the empty ache
would leave….
Then
I can think….

Orbs of silence
  echo
    within
Screaming emptiness
  death-still
    din.
Loneliness
    … aching…
  volcanic turmolt,
Scratching
    glass cages…
  no exits out.
Cul-du-sac highways,
  alleys of
    pain
pull yourself up…
  to be felled
    twice again.
Icy God fingers
  that slip
    through your hands;
reaching….
    seeking…
  in desolation lands.
Unending circles
  down spirals
  of dreams
grasping confusion….
why
  me
    again?

You say
    you want
    "your family" back.
We are not
    "your family"
We have never been
    "your family".
A family…
        shares together
            grows together
    has common bonds…
        common goals.
Stands together
    ..in the good times
    ..and the bad times
They are a unit,
        inseperable,
        welded.
No….
    You can't have
        "your family"
            back
You never had one
    to get back.

Well here I am
        again Lord
full circle
back where I started
……..alone
But I'm not going to panic
    this time
I'm going to trust you…..
            go forward………..
        become stronger
            …….grow
You're all I need Lord!
With You at my side
    I'm going to make it
        I know I am!

CHAPTER 7
BEGINNING TO FLOWER

When I was
            sixteen,
    I was a wife.
When I was nineteen
    ... a mother.
By the time
    I was twenty-nine
    I'd had five children....
    and a husband
    who had a problem
    with alcohol.
Now I'm thirty-six
    and a mother of six...
divorced and on my own;
    and for the first time
in my life
    I'm finding out
who I
    really am.

Shades
   of
      dusky
           dawn
covering
    my
       soul
praying
   for
     the
        sun
to
  break
    through.
Tarpaper
    twilight
    searching for
    the
      bright
         star
   hiding in
       the
         shadows.
Somewhere
    within the caccoon
   the
     butterfly
       awaits
    &&
above
  the clouds
    eternity
      glitters.

(continue on next page)

A
  heartbeat
          away
                  lies
    the
        dream
            fulfilled....
Beyond
    the
        breaking
                dawn......

God of light
   Who dispels all darkness.....
let your light shine
   in me!

Fill the
   darkest corridors
      of my soul
with the radiance
   of your love.

Let the sunshine
   of Your wisdom
   dissolve all confusion
and the promise
   of Your faithfulness
         all fear!

Only by thy
      great mercy
      oh God
   am I
      where I am
                today.
Only by thy
      grace
   am I
      sitting at the foot
      of thy throne.
Only by thy
      hand
   am I
      not in rebellion
         to your holiness.
Help me
      to always remember
      Lord,
   when I look
      at others
      &
      think to judge,

that I am not
      where they are----
         only because of
               thy mercy!

In the darkest caverns
            of confusion
..............a lantern shines
In the deepest depths
            of despair
....................a hand reaches

When all seems lost
      the beacon flashes
And the love of God is there.

In rocky crags
      of disillusion
...........a twine appears
In the dankest pits
      of blank reclusion
............an arm encircles.

When hope is gone
      The Giver gives
And the love of God remains!

CHAPTER 8
JUST ME!

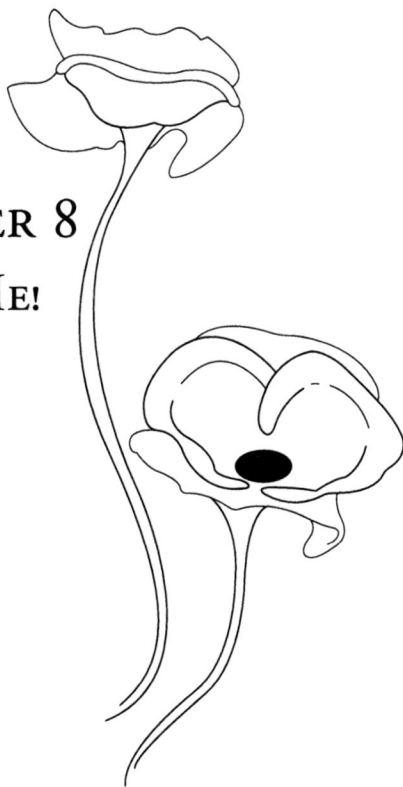

Here it is folks!
  The chance of a lifetime!

One 1949 (slightly used) brunette.
  5ft.4in.(and ½)
    122 lbs. (125..)
    hazel eyes (behind glasses)
      in early thirties (give or take a few years)
Nice to be around
        (when she's sleeping)
  sparkling personality
        (like wine
                ...fizzes out when left out too
long)
    kind nature
        (the kind you're not sure of)
Comes fully equiped with four children
        (living at home)
    and one optional
        (living away from home).
Enjoys activity
    (turning t.v. channel)
  and is a fine cook
    (speciallizes in Kraft macaroni & cheese
dinners)

Can be seen anytime
    (between dusk and twilight).
Don't miss this fine offer, folks....
      sure to be gone quick
          (hopefully)
call 000-HELP!

I am...
   a philosopher
         of life
   a dreamer of dreams
   a poet.
I believe in God
   yet fight Him
     all the way...
I love His word
   yet reject it
       over and over.
I am...
   a seeker
    of all
   a quester of truth
   a hermit
     a spirit.
I love and share
   yet hold my innermost being
       in confined seclusion
I am...
   a stranger in the world
    yet at home
        everywhere.
I am...
   so many
     conflictions....
I am
   just
    .....me.....

My Daddy
    was twelve feet tall
      with a voice
            that boomed
      over mountains
He sang me songs
    explained the angels
            and yodeled.
I'd say
    "Daddy…
            do you love me?"
My Dad
    was eight feet tall
    with a voice
            that boomed
      over my insecurities.
He hollered
    & disapproved
    & hurt me.
I'd say
    "Dad…
    why don't you love me anymore?"

My Father
    is six feet tall
    with a voice
            that's nothing extraordinary.
He sings songs
    talks about
            ordinary things
               & yodels.
I say
    "Dad…
    I love you
    & I know
    you love me too…
            …in your own way."

Alone and scared…
     a tender fifteen,
               she stands.
Her swollen, misshapen stomach protruding…
     aching legs & feet
               unrelenting back-stabbings,
facing an unsympathic world;
She wonders…
     "Is it worth it?"
               ****

Her lythe, young body
     supple and straight again…
                              though stretch-mark
scarred
She clutches a childs
               grimy hand.
Dinner to cook, tears to dry, stamping feet
                              to still,
               bone-weary…
                    from burdensome duties….
     she lifts her cranky bundled babe;
She ponders….
     "Is it worth it?"
               ****

The years gone past…
     her child a teen;
arguing, pouting, screeching hurts…..
                    aimed at her….
she does her mundane chores;
               with no reward;
egg-walking by a sullen off-spring…
               who stomps about self-pityingly;
                    (continue on next page)

And she wonders…..
    "Is it worth it?"
          ****

Her wrinkled, creased face…
        breaking broadly into smiles;
    she caresses her grandchilds buttercup
fingers,
          & tossles her golden-spun hair
    while she cradles the babe
            in her lap.
Her daughter….
    now full-grown….
    kisses her brow
       & says,
    "Thanks Mom, for everything!"
And she says,
    Positively ---
    Without a doubt----
"It was worth it!"

Where was I living......
               before your tummy?
and did you know
      you'd be my mommy?
If God made me.............
      who made Him?
and is a wee little lie
      really a sin?
What would have happened.....
   if you didn't marry Dad......
would I still have been
      the baby you had?
And if you weren't you....
   and he wasn't he...
      then who would I be
      if I didn't be me??

A little boy
        died today.
One minute
        he was riding along
                on his bike,
        and the next
                minute.....
My heart ached;
        I saw his
                mothers face....
                ****

I was complaining today;
        .. the kids are always
                fighting...
        .. they never clean up
                after themselves.
        ..boy, do I need
                a break....
Lord, forgive me,
        I didn't mean
                to take them
                        for granted!
I love them so much!
        Let me enjoy
        and cherish
        each day,
                each minute,
        I have with them....
Because
        you just
                never know.....

Sometimes
        when I'm hurt
                or lonely
                        or scared
I want to run
        to my Momma
        & say
                "kiss it better Momma
                make the hurt go away!
I pick up the phone
        and start
                to dial
then think
"How silly....
        Mommas aren't magic,
                they can't really
                        kiss hurts
                & make them
                                disappear"
or
....can they?
"Kiss it better
&
make it go away....
        o.k.
                Momma..."

You have been
    a blessing
            to me
    ....so many times!
You have always
            been there
whenever I've needed you.
Your friendship
            has been
    a gift...
            from God
                    to me.
    and I'm grateful.
You are
    very special
and I'm so glad
    I know you!

Thanks for being my friend!

When my mother
    was the age
        I am now
        &
I was that
    peculiar age
I wondered
    who she was,
        &
I couldn't understand
the person who
    nagged,
        scolded,
            complained
    &
never seemed to smile.
I hated her
    ferociously
    &
loved her
    with a passion,
    this
        indiscernible
          woman.
Now I'm the age
    my mother was
with a daughter
    that
        peculiar
          age
    &
I understand.
It makes me think
    that just maybe
she
    understood too.

God,
   I'm really
         scared!
Please don't let
   this thing
         f
            a
               l
                  l
                     !
I'm ready
   to come home, Lord
anytime
   you say.....
But please
   just don't
      let it be
         now..

It makes sense...
    totally logical...
        all thought out...
I'm sure I'm right...
    I've checked all the angles.
It makes perfect
        and complete
            SENSE!
So why can't
    anyone else
        see it!?....

I look at
  The stars.
         Lord;
And I see
  your beauty.
I look at
  Jesus;
And I see
  your love.
I look at
  The cross;
And I see
  you compassion.

.......what do you see, Lord
       when You
              look at me?

I always wanted
    … so badly…
to be perfect.
I thought
    that way
    everyone would love me
    & accept me…
but then
    I failed;
and I felt so very bad.
I was ashamed
            and hurt
and felt I was a disappointment;
   but I tried
      to pull myself
            up again
and on I went….
    then…
I failed again.
I made
    bad decisions
    had wrong motives
    jumped ahead
                too fast
    and failed
It was so hard
    to face anyone…
to admit to it…
    to have my pride stomped again.
I really didn't mean
    to shut you out….

(continue on next page)

I just felt foolish,
    and ashamed
… and a failure!
I'm sorry
    if I hurt you….
Please try
    to understand
        and forgive my pride

The tree's majestically
     raises their arms
          to heaven
in the complete abandon
          of adoration.
We bow our heads
               sedately
     glancing discretely
               to see
                    who's watching.
The flowers
     in all their glory
          raise shining faces
               to their maker
openly, freely, full of love.
We fold our hands
               and quietly
                    mumble
     secretly
          peeking
to see
     who's
          watching.
What a paradox....
that God's greatest glory
     man uniquely created
          made in His image
is the only one
     who knows not how
          or cares not how
               to praise his God
                    accordingly.

Sometimes
    I feel so ungrateful;
        I forget all the blessings
    you've given me.

Most-times
    I forget to be thankful;
        for my health & freedom
    my family & friends.

Always
    I take you for granted
        your forgiveness, your peace,
    your protections, your love.

    …Forgive me Lord,
        and make me more aware..

Encased in a self-imposed prison,
  The victim of a scarred soul
    Wracked with pain and mistrust,
      and not understanding…
                                why.

Clouded by long past memories
  of an abused psyche
    unwilling to believe
      in love and compassion.

Down-trodden, discouraged
  not comprehending
    the joy of life….
      of being loved.
  …how sad…

Oh God of love, understanding and compassion
  Let me be a vessel to show forth your love.
    continually, unabatedly
      until it totally encompasses;
        melting, thawing
  ….frozen hearts
  ….frigid fears
  ….and abused dreams.

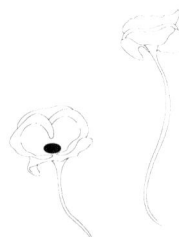

I feel so
        bad for you;
sitting there
        going through
    what I went through.
I wish I
        could help you...
    take some of your
                    pain,
share with you
        some of the things
        I've learned
comfort you....
        but I can't.
You wouldn't accept it
        from me.
My heart aches
    with your
        pain...
and it hurts
    all the worse
        because
I can't help you
    with it...

Please Lord,
    do what I
    can't do.

I've often wondered
    ....and pondered & thought
of who I might be.

If mom hadn't married my dad
    ....like she did
would somebody else have been me?

When I'm lying in bed
phrases run through my head
and I think I might be quite a poet

But when I awaken
my faith in me's shaken
cause the rhymes are all gone,
    wouldn't you know it!

I thought I might write
something casual and light
or even something quite witty;

But all that I got
was a page full of rot
and the result is this dumb little ditty.

Lord,
Help me to be loving
and kind
and considerate.

Lord,
Help me to love
from my heart
..not my ego.

Lord,
Help me to be like you
..loving you
and loving others
through you!

What a wonderful feeling
            to know that
no matter how bad
            things look.......
      You're in control.
No matter how deep
the pit....
      You're there.
No strife, no sorrow,
            no worries
            or cares
   That You can't handle.
It's wonderful to know
   that You can
   take care
            of it all.

Thanks Lord!

Oh God
  of
Abraham, Isaac,
    Jacob
        and me;
How great you are!
I forget
  so often
      your majesty…
Your love
  and power
  overwhelm me!
Lowly sinner
  …failure
      that I am…
you love me
  and
    keep me.
What a great price
  you paid
      for me!
How great are
      your ways
How wonderful
      your plans.
My God….
  My salvation….
Your hands uphold me
  Your truth sustains me.
How high
  above the heavens
      are your ways.

(continue on next page)

I praise you
     my God!
Your ways lead
     to paths
       of
     everlasting joy!

CHAPTER 9
IN THE END

Father
   You know the hearts
      desires
and You delight
   in giving Your children the
          best.
Thankyou
   that in the end
      You gave me
        the best..........

Thankyou
   For the gift of love
      and the joy of finding
        someone to share it with!

In the quite stillness of the night
　　I feel your warmth…
I reach out to touch you
　　and say a quiet prayer
　　　　of thanksgiving
　to have you next to me.
In morning light I gaze
　　upon your beautiful face
　　My heart full of love
　　　　　My soul filled with gratitude
　　　　　　　to have you near
　　　and to know
　　　　　you're mine.
Every minute….every hour
　　　I in wonder stand
　　　　　over-flowing with love
　　　and gratefulness
　to be the one standing at your side.
Always
　　upon my lips
　　　　this silent prayer.….

Thankyou God
　　for such great blessings…
Thankyou God
　　for my wonderful, wonderful
　　　　husband!

I always prayed for......
    I always dreamed of........
        finding someone
           who would
.....cherish me
 ......love me
    ....share life
     with me.

Someone who would be there
    for me.
someone who would
    expect the best
        from me....
and encourage me
    to give it.

Someone who would
    accept me
      for myself......

And motivate me to be
    the most I could be
      ....in myself

Someone giving and kind
    unselfish and gentle
someone who would love me.......
    someone who cared.

    Someone just exactly
      like
        You!

Out of the darkness
    came a light....
from the downpour
    a rainbow.
Into emptiness
    there was being
    and shadows
        disappeared.
How lovely
    was the joy
delight and laughter
    filling the soul.
For out of the night
    day broke
and into my life
    ....came you!

Stay with me
　　because that's where
　　　you want to be,
not because
　　　you feel duty-bound
　　　　　or obligated.
Please me
　　because it pleases you
　　　to do so.
Don't change for me
　　but rather
　　　bend with me
　　　　with the winds
　　　　　of my spirit.
Love me
　　and let me love you
　　　& be free in that,
　　for if love
　　　is not freely given
　　　　it is not truly
　　　　　love.
I give you my heart
　　　&
　　my life,
It is yours
　　for as long
　　　as you want it.
Be happy
　　for that's the only way
　　　you can make me
　　　really happy!

I lived
    in your dreams
    before we met
    and
in my soul
  dwelt an emptiness
    waiting to be filled.

God, in his heaven,
    smiled
knowing what would be…
    knowing the dream
      about to be fulfilled
    and the emptiness
      ready to be overflowed.
"Patience", He whispered..
    and set all
      in motion.

In time
    all was planned.
    What was to be….
          became
    and God
          smiled
and was pleased.

He gave His children
    the best….
    the very best….
    there was!

About the Author

This is my first book.

I've had poetry published in 2 books previously and have written articles for a newspaper many years ago.

I am married to my most wonderful husband, Ken, and we are raising 2 grandchildren.

I have 6 children and 11 grand-children.

I wrote this book because I want young women who are experiencing depression, doubt, fear, loneliness and helplessness to know that there is a light at the end of the tunnel....to just hang on ..... things will get better! You are not alone!

CPSIA information can be obtained at www.ICGtesting.com
Printed in the USA
LVOW11s2156060415

433475LV00001B/363/P